Phoebe Gilman

The Wonderful Pigs of Jillian Jiggs

Scholastic Canada Ltd.

Toronto New York London Auckland Sydney
Mexico City New Delhi Hong Kong Buenos Aires

The Jillian Jiggs books:

Jillian Jiggs
The Wonderful Pigs of Jillian Jiggs
Jillian Jiggs to the Rescue
Jillian Jiggs and the Secret Surprise
Jillian Jiggs and the Great Big Snow

The illustrations for this book were created in gouache on Arches watercolour paper.
The type was set in 16 point American Typewriter.

Scholastic Canada Ltd.
604 King Street West, Toronto, Ontario M5V 1E1, Canada

Scholastic Inc.
557 Broadway, New York, NY 10012, USA

Scholastic Australia Pty Limited
PO Box 579, Gosford, NSW 2250, Australia

Scholastic New Zealand Limited
Private Bag 94407, Greenmount, Auckland, New Zealand

Scholastic Children's Books
Euston House, 24 Eversholt Street,
London NW1 1DB, UK

Copyright © 1988 by Phoebe Gilman.
All rights reserved.

No part of this publication may be reproduced or stored in a retrieval system, or transmitted in any form or by any means, electronic, mechanical, recording, or otherwise, without written permission of the publisher, Scholastic Canada Ltd., 604 King Street West, Toronto, Ontario M5V 1E1, Canada. In the case of photocopying or other reprographic copying, a licence must be obtained from Access Copyright (Canadian Copyright Licensing Agency), 1 Yonge Street, Suite 800, Toronto, Ontario M5E 1E5 (1-800-893-5777).

National Library of Canada Cataloguing in Publication

Gilman, Phoebe, 1940-2002.
The wonderful pigs of Jillian Jiggs / Phoebe Gilman.

ISBN 0-439-96186-6

I. Title.

PS8563.I54W6 2004   jC813'.54
C2004-901753-5

7 6 5   Printed in Singapore   07 08 09   ISBN-10 0-439-96186-6 / ISBN-13 978-0-439-96186-8

A long time ago, as you may recall,
Jillian Jiggs never cleaned up at all.

"Jillian, Jillian, Jillian Jiggs,
It looks like your room has been lived in by pigs!"

Well, wonder of wonders, without any warning,
Jillian cleaned up one Saturday morning.

She made her room tidy and neat as a pin.
''Can this really be Jillian's room that I'm in?''

Jillian smiled, then she looked all around.
"Now where is that jar full of buttons I found?

Look at these buttons," said Jillian Jiggs.
"Don't they look just like the noses of pigs?"

"We'll make little pigs and then set up a store.
I'm sure we can sell at least fifty or more.

We'll make lots of money, we'll be billionaires!
Then Mother can rest and forget all her cares."

Once Jillian started, she zipped right along,
Turning out piggies while singing this song:

"Jillian, Jillian, Jillian Jiggs,
Maker of wonderful, marvelous pigs!"

The first little pig had a sweet smiling face.
The second she dressed up in old-fashioned lace.

And then she decided to give them both names.
She called one Clarissa, the other one James.

The next little pig had a hat and a cane.
His name was George and his girlfriend was Jane.

Miranda had red cheeks and long, dark eyelashes.
McTavish was old and had drooping mustaches.

She made up a pirate pig, Blackberry Billy,
To play with her princess pig, Lavender Lilly.

"Jillian, Jillian, Jillian Jiggs,
Maker of wonderful, marvelous pigs!"

A striped pig named Dudley, a plaid pig named Sue.

A family of Martian pigs, Beep, Bop and Boo.

She might still be sitting there, sewing away,
Except Rachel and Peter came over to play.

"Hi, Rachel! Hi, Peter! Quick, come on in.
Guess what I'm making," she said with a grin.

They couldn't believe it—pigs, pigs galore,
Were scattered all over the bed, desk and floor.

"Jillian, Jillian, Jillian Jiggs,
Your room <u>really</u> looks like it's lived in by pigs!"

They gathered them up and they took them all out.
They made up a sign and they marched all about.

"Jillian, Jillian, Jillian Jiggs,

Maker of wonderful, marvelous pigs!

Ten cents a pig, not one penny more.
They're waiting for you at Jillian's store."

21

They came to buy pigs. They came by the dozens.
Brothers and sisters, best friends and cousins.

Was Jillian happy?

Now here's a sad tale.

How could she put all her pigs up for sale?

"Oh, no, not Marlene! She's so cute and so cuddly.

And not my Clarissa or Rosie or Dudley.

I can't give up Marvin, he'd miss his friend Thomas.
I'll never sell him, I gave him my promise.

No, no, not McTavish, I can't let <u>him</u> go.
And Blackberry Billy would miss me, you know.

I can't sell poor Gregory, he has the flu.
He should stay in bed for the next day or two.

29

I simply can't do it. It's over. I'm through..."

Then all of a sudden she knew what to do.

"Step right up, friends! Have lots of fun!
Sew your own pigs! Learn how it's done!

We'll make hundreds and millions and zillions of pigs!"

said wonderful, marvelous Jillian Jiggs.

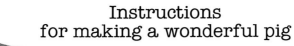

Instructions
for making a wonderful pig

Materials

Old stocking . . . . any color. Wonderful pigs come in all colors!

Needle and thread . . . . to sew your pig.

Polyester fiberfill . . . . for stuffing. You wouldn't want a skinny pig!

Embroidery floss . . . . to sew your pig's eyes and mouth.

Felt . . . . .to make ears so that your pig can hear you.

Yarn . . . . .unless you want a bald pig.

Button . . . . for your pig's nose.

Pipe cleaners . . . . if your pig is a Martian pig.

Lace and ribbon . . . . for a fancy pig.

Pink crayon . . . . for coloring rosy cheeks on your pig.

Scissors and glue

running stitch whip stitch

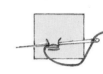

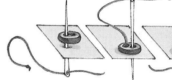
fastening thread sewing on a button

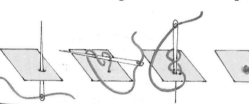
french knot

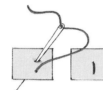
surprised mouth

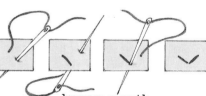
happy mouth

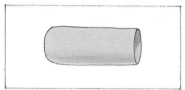

1. Cut one piece of stocking 25 cm (10") long.

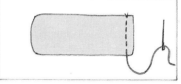

2. Sew a row of running stitches around one end of the stocking.

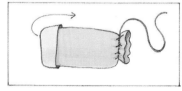

3. Pull thread tight to gather. Fasten and cut thread, then turn the stocking inside-out.

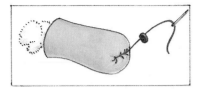

4. Stuff the head with fiberfill. Sew a button on in the middle of the stitching line.

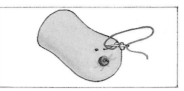

5. Bring the needle and embroidery floss up from the inside and sew french knots for the eyes.

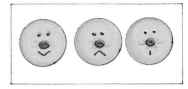

6. Sew a happy or mad or surprised mouth.

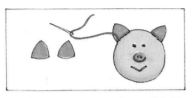

7. Cut two triangles of felt for the ears.
Use the whip stitch to sew them in place.

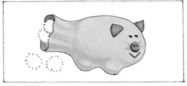

8. Add more stuffing for the body, placing four balls of stuffing inside, underneath, for the feet.

9. Tie thread around the balls from outside to complete the feet.

10. Twist the remainder of stocking to make a curly tail.

11. Tie the end in a knot.

Glue or sew on yarn or fiberfill for hair, mustaches or beards. Add ribbon and lace for fancy pigs. Poke in bits of pipe cleaner for Martian pigs. Color your pig's cheeks rosy.

Give your pig a name and say, "Welcome to my family!"